Thomas B. Peacock

The Rhyme of the Border War

A historical poem of the Kansas-Missouri guerrilla war, before and during the late

rebellion, the principal character being the famous guerrilla, Charles William

Quantrell

Thomas B. Peacock

The Rhyme of the Border War
*A historical poem of the Kansas-Missouri guerrilla war, before and during the late rebellion,
the principal character being the famous guerrilla, Charles William Quantrell*

ISBN/EAN: 9783337272531

Printed in Europe, USA, Canada, Australia, Japan

Cover: Foto ©Andreas Hilbeck / pixelio.de

More available books at **www.hansebooks.com**

THE RHYME

OF

THE BORDER WAR.

A HISTORICAL POEM

OF THE

KANSAS-MISSOURI GUERRILLA WAR,

BEFORE AND DURING THE LATE REBELLION,

THE PRINCIPAL CHARACTER BEING

THE FAMOUS GUERRILLA,

CHARLES WILLIAM QUANTRELL.

BY

THOMAS BROWER PEACOCK,

AUTHOR OF

" THE VENDETTA," AND OTHER POEMS.

NEW YORK

G. W. Carleton & Co., Publishers.

MDCCCLXXX.

Stereotyped by
SAMUEL STODDER.
ELECTROTYPER & STEREOTYPER,
90 ANN STREET, N. Y.

TROW
PRINTING AND BOOK-BINDING CO.
N. Y.

TO

I. E. P.

" None without hope e'er loved the brightest fair,
But Love can hope where Reason would despair."
—*Lyttelton.*

CONTENTS.

THE RHYME

OF

THE BORDER WAR.

CANTO I.

INTRODUCTORY.

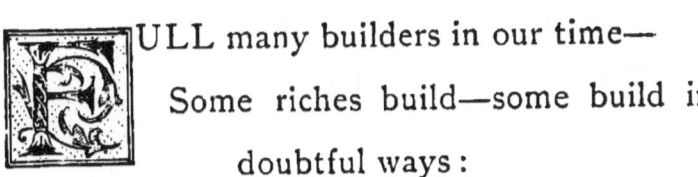 ULL many builders in our time—

Some riches build—some build in

doubtful ways :

I build the fair and lofty rhyme,

Of deeds heroic sing the praise.

'Though now I touch the breathing lyre,

To sing past war, if of those days

Should other harps than mine aspire,

It boots not who best wears the bays—

So that the poem hath expressed

The music of the poet's breast

With feeling that to time imparts

A light of pathos melting hearts—

That mystic power of poesy,

Defineless as the Deity—

I sing as now my whim suits best,

And leave to man and time the rest.

I sing of war—red cruel war,

The desperate deeds of desperate men—

Of war, whose echoes yet afar

Low thunder over hill and plain.

.   .   .   .   .   .

Lo ! see excited cities stir !

See the deserted shop and field !

What in man's history doth occur ?

To what doth fruitful toil now yield ?

His iron front grim-visaged War

Doth bold display with wrath unmeet!—

Arisen, Mars' fierce, lurid star,

And Battle stamps his bloody feet!

O! to what ominous shadows dark

Time's finger points with awful meaning!

Hark! the future stricken groan! hark!

The widow's wail and young babe she is
    weaning!

.   .   .   .   .   .

O Kansas! land of many a change!

Land of promise! land of fairest things!

Where war and carnage oft did range

Now Peace and Beauty spread their wings.

Once thou wert a dense, dark wilderness,

When the Red Man monarch ruled,

Till Pike of Pike's Peak came to bless

Thee, Kansas!—soon the White Man schooled.

The school was rough at first, for those

Who followed erst the bold Pike west,

Were nigh as savage as their foes,

The Aborigines, at best—

When the Bowie and revolver ruled,

And men alone in these were schooled.

Here the Border Ruffian came—

Here the early pioneer

Found the Missourian would defame

With slavery the whole frontier.

At Lecompton, which now lies

In mouldering ruins 'neath the skies,

'Twas Judge Lecompte who first essayed

To hold a court upon thy soil,

And though he coaxed and swore and prayed,

Thy land was shamed by many a broil.

Here John Brown, the fanatic, made

A name which few this day admire ;

And Jim Lane here his powers displayed

In orations touched with fire.

Here bold Montgomery led his men

Like Roderick Dhu through Scotia's glen;

Though now his pen supplants his sword,

Then Anthony* a fighter warred.

Here journalism first betrayed

The hope the law would be obeyed

Through *Herald,*† *Free-State*—Speer's *Tribune,*

Which bloomed a flower that perished soon.

Then thy first bard, Realf,‡ did essay

The Muse—his poems seem like day

Amid that one dark night of time,

When all was vengeance, hate and crime.

All through thy Border-Ruffian days

I find more to condemn than praise—

When Territory and when State

First dawned—a thing of fate—

When Governor Reeder saw death near,

When Shannon ruled the hour in fear—

* Col. D. R. Anthony, Editor *Leavenworth Times.*
† i.e., *Herald of Freedom.*   ‡ Richard Realf.

One for his life compelled to fly,

One to resign compelled, or die;

While Robinson and other men

Who Kansas served as rulers then,

Got little to repay the trust

Save hope, which oft deludes, and must.

Thank God! they've passed—the wagon wheel

Gives place to iron trail and steel.

Thy Santa Fé and Pacific roads—

Thy Fort Scott lines, and more to come,

Have added thousands of abodes,

For many thus found thee a home.

True literature soars on the wing—

Thine own—with beauty none deny—

Thy poets, lark-like, sweetly sing—

Thy authors in their field are high—

On thy soil, Smith,* of Greeley tie,

---

* Nicholas Smith, the talented writer, formerly a resident of Leavenworth, who married Miss Ida Greeley, eldest daughter of Horace Greeley.

First wrote tales which do time defy.

O Kansas! thou hast wonders seen,

While Territory and a State!

Thou art, like mortal man, I ween,

A creature led by tyrant fate!

Here white men drive the red man back,

To be supplanted by the black;

Though now and then, a moment seen,

The strange wild Indian of the plain,

His star is setting low between

The Rocky Mountains and the main.

His fate and the buffalo's are one—

They gather to the setting sun.

O Kansas! may you ever be

A thing of beauty and of love,

Where all the God-like angels see

Hope, Joy and Peace, from their high homes
    above.

.   .   .   .

The maiden Morn walks with the Hours,

Their tread has wakened all the flowers

That now are smiling sweet and fair,

And whispering unto God in prayer—

Bright birds of beauty welkin wing,

And matin-hymns to Heaven do sing;

The east with great omnipotent power,

Burns with the breath of God this hour!

That mystery of life—oh, strange bequeath!—

That hems man in from birth till death,

And aught he knows e'en further still,

Broods in the vale and on the hill!

A cottage sweetly veiled in vine

Of ivy, myrtle, and woodbine,

Stands fair with portal open wide,

Where two stand talking, side by side—

A lovely woman, sweet and young,

A man who looks from greatness sprung—

Stand with a something in their eyes,

Which tells that gloomy darkness lies

Deep in their hearts : " O husband dear,

I tremble with my fearful fear !"

Her pure frank eyes are bent on his—

Sweet sunbeams in a sea of dawn—

When by his side all hours were bliss,

When parted, life 'mid clouds dragg'd on,

" Oh ! have no fear !—hope, hope !" he said ;

" Hope that we meet ere moon hath fled !"

" The spring-flower blooming sweet and dear,

Is hope without one sorrow near,

But when 'tis smote by chilling frost,

'Tis blasted hope forever lost !"

She quickly, earnestly replies,

With anxious looks and plaintive sighs.

" Th' Union I go to help restore !—

And O ! 'tis hard to leave thee for the war !

But my country calls, and go I must !

The duty's hard, but it is just !

2

And Kansas, our own home and State,

Is threatened with Guerrilla hate!"

He said, and kissed her rose lips dewed with
    wine—

The wine of love and beauty sweet—

She looked so fair she seem'd divine—

An angel strayed from near God's feet.

He long caressed her with a sigh,

Said "God bless you, darling wife, good-by."

Then vaulting on his steed he cried :

"Farewell!" and then away did ride.

A sweet solitude of flowers rare,

Blushed sweetly in the valley fair ;

But not so sweet as Ida Vane,

The young bride whose bright hopes did wane.

As innocent she looked to be,

There blushing 'mid the woodland bowers,

As fair young children playfully

Strewing early spring-time flowers.

So fair, so young, this one-week bride,

Thus soon put from her husband's side—

Like early dawn upon the lake,

She rested on the heart of God—

She knew He would not her forsake

Nor her Willie who 'midst dangers trod—

Afar in war's dread battles wild,

Where death exulted in his power ;

She had a woman's love, a child

In years—but fourteen times spring's flower

Had bloom'd since first she'd breathed the air

Of a world of sorrow and despair.

" Dear God ! from Thy high home above

Bend low and hear me, please !

Dear God !" she cried, " preserve my Love,

In war where death 's in every breeze !

Dear God ! I pray thee, guard mine own

Dear Willie while away from me—

Please bring him back ere flowers now grown

Have faded to eternity!

Dear God, where Willie e'er doth rove,

I ask but this, O God!—[she on her knees]—

Dear God! from Thy high home above

Bend low and hear me, please!"

Thus prayed this fair wife, innocent

And young—too young for such great cares;

And yet, midst all the worst, low bent,

God hears and heeds such earnest prayers.

A bay-flower glowed in beauty fair

From out the midnight of her hair—

The wine of beauty in her face,

Within her eye the wine of love—

The wine of all we love to trace

In woman—virtues from above—

Was hers, the lovely Ida Vane's,

One week ago fair Ida Bell,

But William Vane her heart obtains—

The fairest girl in all the dell:

Her bosom glowed with love as bright,

As light of stars a cloudless night—

And like those sweet immortal flowers,

True woman's love grows on sublime—

Like them it soars o'er mortal hours—

It lives beyond the bounds of time!

Unto the young wife, through her near

And heavy, sorrowing, sickening fear,

All is lost 'though beautiful nature here.

Lo! see yon lucid lake—so clear!—

Where lilies with their satin-stars

Wave sweetly in the breezes here,

With snowy beauty, nothing mars!

Near by the gold-eyed king-cup glows,

With purple clover and red rose,

Where flower-cradled, golden bees,

Sway to and fro unto the breeze,

With arrowy sweep a river glides

'Twixt hills, then flows on dreamily,

Where beauteous fish flash sparkling sides,

There sporting in the waters free.

The vales where doth God's grace appear,

The sylvan wilds—hills, forests here,

Invite the wanderer to draw near—

Voices of mysterious beauty breathe

Adown the lonely lovely vale !—

'Twould seem that unseen angels wreathe

A crown of glory in the dale,

For some good being of this world,

And whisper of the boon impearled !

Here countless fragrant flame-like flowers

In beauty bloom 'round wildwood bowers—

Here birds of beauty breast the breeze,

And hide amid the leafy trees,

And sing a lovely madrigal,

While each dear little heart is full.

The music of sweet, hidden hours,

The poesy of fairest flowers,

Were here — sweet breathing through the
    bowers—
Too, the Silences their Sabbath keep,
Far, far within the forest deep.
As blushing to her bridal bed
The young bride walks in beauty fair.
With modest fears that she is wed
Yet joyous, for her heart is there—
Glides day's lingering sweet twilight
Into the chamber of the night.

CANTO II.

QUANTRELL'S EARLY HOME.

THE mansion of the Hildebrand,
 The fairest of Ohio's land,
  Is glowing freely in the night
From a thousand brilliants bright!—
A thousand chandeliers illume
The mystic shadows of the gloom ;
And out the moon—out stars are all—
To help make glad the festival ;
Bright banners float upon the walls,
And happy faces throng the halls—
And sparkling wines flow free as water;
And every neighboring son and daughter
Adds to the mirth that ripples here,

Where silence reigned for many a year.

The tables in the banquet hall

Are spread, and dancers to the call

Are lightly tripping to the lutes

Pianos, violins and flutes—

All is wild wassail and good cheer—

They quaff red wine and foaming beer.

Long years agone Hugh Hildebrand

Had left his home and natal land,

To spend the wealth at his command:

The envious whispered, young and old,

Abroad he'd been an outlaw bold—

In foreign lands, in years since fled

And vanished with the other dead.

But where he'd been, what done, how well,

It boots not to this rhyme to tell—

Suffice he'd kept his promise given

Unto a sister saint in Heaven.

That he'd return from foreign joys

To watch and guard her orphan boys—
Charles and Paul, she loved so well,
An invalid, their sire, Quantrell :
Suffice that too he homeward came
His lovely cousin's hand to claim—
The beauteous, radiant Rosalie,
Fairer than brightest star we see,
Sweet as the scent of summer rose
When showers its fairest charms disclose—
As perfect as the angels be
Which work to lessen misery,
As gentle as the rays of love
That light alcoves of Heaven above—
In all, so sweet, so good, so fair,
She seems of neither earth nor air,
But something far too good to be,
Aught save those stainless saints we 'd see
Could we but roam that world so high,
Beyond the borders of the sky.

She, this earth-sprite's happy now,

With rosy cheek and snowy brow :

Oh, she enjoys her hours of glee,

For happy, blithe and joyed is she

As poet—singing unto those

Living in a world of prose—

Bright sees the magic of his powers

In weeds transformed to fairest flowers!

'Tis the fair one's happy wedding night,

And each and every winsome wight

Is blithe and gay, and feels the cheer—

Feels that both life and love are dear.

Each aged servant shares the bliss,

The master's joys are hers and his ;

With ardor like in Eastern land,

Both Rosalie and Hildebrand

They loved with love's mysterious power—

As odors of the fragrant flower

Attract us till their petals blow

In close communion with us: know
Ye that the flower's perfume is love
Escaped from the heart's o'erfilled alcove!
To be imbibed by saintliest thing
Save true hearts with it o'erflowing!
The past seemed living as of yore,
When Hildebrand the elder, bore
The name of being free from care,
And perfectly happy, which is rare—
He masked his heart from them, I'd swear.
With all the wealth that heart can crave,
And generous to a fault, he gave
And squandered like a prince of old—
His heart too warm to e'er grow cold.
Night in and out his halls he'd fill
With friends from many a vale and hill,
Till every marble hall would be
Resounding to the revelry.
Thus he lived his life away

In dissipation mad and gay,

Till death low laid him in his tomb,

When silence did his mansion gloom,

And bats and spiders lined the walls,

And phantoms walked his silent halls.

Night waxed and waned, and Morning fair,

A maid of beauty, loosed her hair

Ere all the guests had left the scene,

Where dance and song and wine, I ween,

Were plenty.—Thus and thus again,

Like his mad sire, the son insane

Pursued this wild destructive course,

Which had its end in time perforce.

His Rosalie, a flower too frail

For earth, now bloomed in Heaven's sweet vale,

Where God did place her to earth's cost

Ere the life-spark of her soul was lost—

This the cause that Hugh so reckless went

The course his sire had madly bent.

Hugh hung a garland of love and flowers

Over her grave so sad and lone—

He wept for her and the happy hours

That beyond the silent stars had flown.

Fortune wrecked, Hildebrand thought best,

With his two nephews, to go West,

And their sire, who this wish expressed—

To take another name and try

To work once more to fortune high.

His nephews both—the Quantrell twins—

Charles and Paul, well knew his sins—

Well knew his woes, and pitied well

He who from Heaven had plunged to Hell.

CANTO III.

LULU EARL.

O ! yonder comes the sylph of morn—
A maiden young, sweet, wondrous
fair ;
'Tis Lulu Earl, whose charms adorn
The wilds, and breathe a glory everywhere—
An unkissed virgin, fair and dear,
Whose knowledge of earth's sin confess'd,
Was nothing—for her soul was clear
As young babe on its mother's breast.
The radiant angels breathed her name,
For e'en in Heaven they felt the flame
Her soul sent outward everywhere ;
She was so fair that if man glanced

Upon her he would be entranced,

And covet her for his sweet bride—

And who could blame him!—who could chide

The wish to own the flower of Heaven,

God loaned at morn to take ere even?

And there was cause too for alarm!—

From human vipers which earth swarm—

If God in vain shields with His arm.

The lily roundness of her arm,

The tempting beauty of her form

And face might bring this fair one harm—

For many are less good than warm.

Far, far within the hidden vale

Where she knew nothing save the good,

There is on earth no nobler tale

Than her life and those in that wildwood,

Where her, fair Lulu's, presence gave

A happiness most only dream

This cheerless side of the still grave—

She was God's chosen Heaven-sent beam—

She was the poet's ideal maid,

Who comes like moon from midnight shade,

Who makes bright even dark despair—

O God ! Thou knowest she was fair !

In her sweet home—a forest bower—

She blushed, the wildwood's loveliest flower.

God secretes in places lone and still

The rarest products of His will;

For contact with the world disarms

His fairest flowers of half their charms.

.　　　.　　　.　　　.　　　,

A storm howls like a fiend in pain ;

In swaying fury falls the rain ;

Around spreads out the forest black :

Above extends the roaring wrack—

And oft deep voices muttering call,

As through Plutonian darkness fall

The voices of the damn'd and lost,

3

Whose crimes the love of God hath cost!

Who wander boundless deeps of Hell,

Plunged in vast wastes of darkness fell.

The hills unloose their shadows vast,

Which wander down the angry blast.

A sound—as when God's voice doth sweep

Through space's vast and awful deep

In mighty thunder, whose great voice awes

The Powers He tells t' obey His laws—

Now bellows, thundering loud and far—

Heard by Peri on remotest star;

All objects by the storm are hurl'd

As though an earthquake shakes the world.

Through swaying trees, o'er crushed flower,
thyme,

Upon a steed as black as crime,

A horseman lone pursues his way,

Hoping that some shelter may

Be found :—lo ! the lightning's glare

Shows him a cottage closed with care.

" Thank God !" he said—" Heaven must be
    near,

Though Hell's abroad ; it would appear,

For demons of most fearful fright

Seem'd galloping around this night,

Until this cottage fair and bright

Seems to have vanished ghouls of night,"

He said.   " Had I shelter for my head,

Methinks I would not ask a bed."

The lightning danced before his eyes,

And seemed to picture Paradise !—

As, drunken with a Heavenly wine,

He fancied things that seemed divine !

A form of flame—a spirit form—

Flashing through the rolling storm,

Called to him from a cloud of fire,

Then vanished in the empyrean higher!

" Methinks a fever racks my brain

Or else I soon will be insane!

For on this night, when Hell's abroad,

I've seen an angel sent by God!"

Lo! yonder comes the gray-eyed Dawn,

And shadows dank float to the woods—

The genii of the storm has gone,

And sought the deepest solitudes.

Weary, hungry, wet all o'er

The storm-benighted traveler drew

His reins before the cottage door,

And loudly cried "Halloo! halloo!"

He hears door-bolts fly back, and now

Sees a fine face and massive brow

Protrude. "Good sir! I shelter seek;

The storm last night has left me weak

And hungry too." "Dismount, good sir!

The best we have with you we'll share!"

The stranger-guest was soon abed,

Asleep and resting; 'neath a shed

His steed—for Earl was good, and sought

To live as Christ his soul had taught;

And all who ever chanced that way

Bless'd Earl and family, and the day

That chanced to cast them in the wood

Where they lived as Christians should.

The day-god, in his golden car,

Had driven down the skies full far,

When he, the stranger-guest, arose,

Donned his late wet, now fire-dried, clothes,

And, looking from his window, starts

At sight of one who deftly parts

The vines of honeysuckles sweet,

As on she glides on music feet,

Like some fair sylph, whose home is far

In fragrant valley of a star.

A fair enchantress sweet she seemed,

Or those that saw when waked still dreamed—

For where she stepped, unto the view,

Sprang flowers early, sweet and new!
And bloomed more beautiful and fair
Than rarest flowers on earth elsewhere.
The blood-red blush of her ripe mouth,
Whereon the grace of beauty dewed,
Like scarlet rose blown from the south
Looked, to the eye of him that viewed.
Oh, quaff the nectar of her lips!
Oh, drink the glory of her eyes!
Oh, young, fresh, beautiful, she sips
The beauty out of Paradise.
How fair!—but oh, she's vanished from his
     sight,
The day so sweet has yielded unto night.
Scarce the stranger-guest his fast had broke
When the maiden's voice the welkin woke!
Joy! the music of her step he hears!
The silken sound of her approach !—
How ecstatic to his ravished ears,

Her coming words can never broach.

She comes, a sweet gift from above—

The beauteous Morning Star of Love!

Though, could he tell as many times

As there are flaming stars in heaven

His thoughts of her in poet's rhymes,

Not half of all his love were given.

She comes! that gushing glory glides

T'ward him, and near him now abides.

The wanton wind has opened rude

Her dress, and laid her bosom nude,

Unknown to her, for she was pure,

And could not such a thing endure.

"Good morning! My name, stranger fair,

Is Quantrell!—for yours ask could I dare?"

Said he, the guest. She blushed: her hair

Vailed much of her sweet, radiant face,

Tossed by the breeze that still kept pace

Full well. "O yes! good sir! mine is Earl,

Lulu Earl.   I trust you will regain

Your strength lost in the storm and rain.

Our home is small, but you are free

To all its space, so easy be."

How fair! how sweet! how strangely dear!

With love's blush mantling on her cheek,

Is she, the gold-haired maid, that here

Stands trembling with a joy unspeak.

That mystery of the soul call'd love glow'd

     bright :

'Twas instant love—'twas love at sight.

Lulu loved the stranger, on her part,

With all the virgin-passion of her heart.

He loved her more than he had dreamed

That he could love—so beautifully she beamed

On him—her Heavenly hazel eyes

Broke on him such a sweet surprise,

He felt as though some Unknown Power

Had placed him in a Heavenly bower,

Where everything far fairer beamed

Than he before had ever dreamed.

Through long exposure Quantrell knew

He needed rest—and it is true

The lovely Lulu cast a spell

Upon him that he knew full well

Held him, charmed him to the spot,

That he long lingered in the grot—

While lovely, loving Lulu fair,

Attended to his wants with care.

When they did part to them 'twas known

That each the other's heart did own.

With kisses which alone love knows,

When the very soul o'erflows,

And with embraces warm and sweet,

As when o'er clouds two angels greet,

They parted with love's deepest vows,

To meet to marry 'neath the boughs

Of her sire's whispering forest trees,

Where the sweetly breathing breeze
Seemed to be a breath from Heaven,
Which God to earth had kindly given.

CANTO IV.

QUANTRELL'S SOLILOQUY.

O! yonder is the king of day
Peeping o'er the forest gray!
Through camp the echoing noises
gay,
Sound as if a gala day.
The soldiers sing the songs they know—
Some are coarse and vile and low,
Some sweet and beautifully flow;
Each more sweet and tender grows,
For here and there love's rebecks rose.
It is the camp of Jennison,
And his men are full of fun
And liquor—for the leader thought

[43]

Those that drank most the better fought.

Lo! who are those two men we trace

There conversing face to face?

'Tis Jennison and him we 've seen

Out in the storm and in the green

And lovely vale—"Now, while away,

I found a spot more fair than day;

And made such friends I ask your aid

That no one harms them in the raid.

Since I have e'er been to you true

This one request I make of you—

Avoid this valley; change your route,

And I will be your faithful scout

As I have been your trusted spy!"

" Impossible, e'en though I try!

For my wild clan will me defy.

My wounds will keep me here for days—

My clan have money sworn to raise—

They know the land where you have been

The richest all the country in.

Since I 'm wounded, sick and sore,

Either you must lead, or Moore.

Since you decline my place to touch,

Because my men have drank too much,

As leader, Moore must act as such.

Although I 'd like your wish to grant

I 'm very much afraid I can't !

Though I promise you that Moore

Will see none harms those you adore !"

Though Quantrell show'd not one alarm,

He resolved to warn his friends of harm—

So from the camp he swiftly flies

On the first steed that met his eyes.

     *   *   *   *   *

" They come ! they come !" said Quantrell low

To all his friends—while foes draw near—

Besides th' Earls—besides her loved so,

Were uncle, father, brother dear.

The foe come on with yell and cry,

But many of the foremost die.

With doors and windows bolted, barred,

In Earl's house the defenders warred.

Here Hildebrand displays a might

In marksmanship that proves his right

As tutor of his nephews—they

E'er as true an aim display.

Their foes still pour from out the woods,

Fierce demons from the solitudes!

Now back, that wild and hellish horde

Seek shelter which the woods afford,

To wait a spell, for night is near,

When they'll attack with less of fear.

Lo! yonder in her pale career,

The moon wheels by each tarrying sphere—

And yonder from the umbrage shade,

Which the oak majestic made,

A form unseen, save by that Eye

That sweeps all space below, on high,

Creeps through the high and thick-grown
    grass,

As a serpent oft will pass,

And lo ! a flame leaps toward the sky !

The door opes and the inmates fly !

On—on they fly—and while they do

Countless rifle-balls pursue—

And while they fly from the murderous lot

Back each man oft sends a vengeful shot.

    *   ·*   *   *   *

Morn dawns ! but oh, an awful morn,

Within the vale of Avadore,

Where Lulu Earl was happy born,

And lived where all was peace before

The hour that brought the murderous band

To rob and slay on every hand.

That band had vanish'd with the night,

Like devils, fearful of the light,

But left behind a woeful sight.

Though their own wounded and their dead

They took with them when they fled,

Here four on farm of Earl are dead,

And here two others freely bled—

And one was very fair—

And one stood o'er her in despair—

For the fair girl on the ground

Lay bleeding from a cruel wound.

'Twas Lulu Earl who lay so weak,

'Twas Quantrell stood, too full to speak.

For the one he loved so well

Was dying from her wound so fell.

Oh, where's a hell sufficient hot

For him that crushes down the good?

The good that die in many a spot

In the dawn of man and womanhood!

"Dear Lulu! Darling of my life,

My heart is broken in the strife,

An I with thy pain, my soul, mine own !"

" Dear Charles ! I'll leave you soon alone !

I soon shall go, but have no fear—

Now opened is my spirit ear !

List ! I hear the music-footed Hours

In endless silence onward go,

And close beside the sylvan bowers,

I hear the lovely flowers grow ;

I hear the ' music of the spheres,'

I hear the angels singing now,

Above the sky, where Christ appears

With pity written on His brow !"

Low Quantrell sank upon his knee,

All heedless of his own wounds sore,

And kiss'd the lips he could not see

For tears that from his eyes do pour,

" Kiss me, dear Charles ! a farewell kiss !"

She smiles, as slowly to the bliss

Of Heaven she goes—she does not groan—

3

She smiles in death, and makes no moan ;

Like soft decline of summer day

She sweetly passed to God away.

As morning mist floats from the sod

Rose her spirit past the stars to God.

All that in life's most wondrous fair,

In death none with her could compare !

" This deep, dread silence ! is it death ?"

Thought Quantrell, with a painful breath.

" Oh, wake ! and feel the breathing morn—

Oh, wake my loved one, wake, dear heart !

Didst thou not tell me, angel-born,

That nevermore we 'd part ?

She wakes not !   God ! can this be death ?"

Close to her heart he placed his head

And listened, holding fast his breath—

Long listened—then cried : " My soul is dead !

O Christ, where art Thou now !" he cried—

" O God, why didst Thou take her from me ?

Why hast Thou me time's joy denied

When she's Thine through all eternity?"

As funeral bells wail for the good

That die in youth, before the dawn

Of manhood and of womanhood,

So mourned Quantrell o'er his Lulu gone.

"All gone! My Lulu gone! Great God!

Is it thus I feel Thy chast'ning rod?

My father, uncle—my Lulu's mother!

And my beloved and only brother!

He with whom I oft have roved,

Whom I loved—aye! more than loved—

Lies stark! his generous spirit fled,

Alas! alas! is dead, is dead!

Oh, was he not myself almost,

When born with me the self-same day!

Methinks I hear his pensive ghost,

That doth to me for vengeance pray;

As there he lies he so like me

Doth look, in every feature free,

Did I not know I live through pain

I 'd swear my very self were slain !

All, all are gone save me forlorn—

Why was I left ? was it to mourn ?"

" No !"   " What voice is that I hear ?"

" To àvenge the dead you're left—

The dead that to you are so dear,

Of whom so ruthlessly you were bereft !"

When that voice died upon his ear,

As "One crying in the wilderness,"

Cried Quantrell, " It is well ! I hear !

I shall avenge you ! ease your wild distress !

Hear me, high Heaven ! O God, me hear !

And ye ! my friends in spirit near,

I shall avenge each, all of you,

And make your murderers bitter rue

The hour they wrought this fearful woe,

In the blood that through their vitals flow !

This tribute to your memory—

To the golden past so sweet to me—

From this time forth I well shall pay,

From morn till night, from night till morn I'll

    slay!

Five thousand men brought on my woes—

Five thousand men make up my foes—

I know them all—each, every one—

And none shall my just vengeance shun!

Five thousand men shall feel my power,

Shall 'neath my hand of vengeance cower!"

CANTO V.

QUANTRELL AND JENNISON.

IS eighteen hundred and sixty-two—
    The north winds pierce the deep
    hills through ;
'Tis September, and the leaves are browned
That fly the breeze, that cover ground,
That droop upon the trees around.
The Missouri river waters flow,
Swollen in their channel go.
A hundred mounted men or more,
Armed to the teeth, are on the shore.
A moving arsenal each seeming,
From the many weapons gleaming
From belts and boot-legs—from the side—

Bristling as they onward ride.

All sudden south their way they take—

All sudden swifter progress make!

Till to farm of Harris they have come

To take the products of his home.

To get by right of might a share

Of the rich farmer's bounteous fare.

At the head of the company

The leader rides, and marked is he

Above the vulgar herd of men—

Above the herd pent in the pen

Of common thoughts and things and ways,

Where one day shows the life of days—

The now repeats the past, tells what's to
   come,

As footsteps sound continual hum.

'Though small of build, one understands

From looks, that he alone commands.

His air and aspect this confess

In language better than words express.

His eyes are blue, the deepest blue,

Almost black they sometimes grew—

'Twas when of wrongs their owner thought,

Of which the bitter past was fraught.

He was not handsome, yet his face

Express'd a strong, strange, winning grace;

His form was sinewy, strong 'though spare—

Wronged, he was a roused lion from his lair.

The flag, born by a war-scarr'd son,

Tells unto each and every one

The chieftain's name—with black background,

The name of " Quantrell," dreaded round.

His hat—each bold, wild follower's too—

Toss'd high a plume of raven hue.

His fierce men no allegiance knew

Save to him who had ta'en them through

All kinds of dangers, wild and dread,

And yet did save them from the dead.

All quailed beneath his eagle eye,

All him obeyed, and asked not why.

They looked upon him as a sage,

The mighty Nestor of his age.

They looked to him as to a god

Who held o'er earth a magic rod—

A potent wizard power, that wrought

Great wonders—with a mystery fraught.

With things mysterious wise he'd grown—

Of the bright stars he'd learned man's fate—

Beyond earth's confines the unknown

He knew, but dared not to relate.

As Napoleon cross'd the Lodi o'er,

With followers that feared at first,

So Quantrell led the way—before

He went—his men following 'gainst the
    worst—

It booted not the odds how great,

They trusted all to him and fate.

3*

He seem'd as cool in battle's roar

As though he walk'd the calm sea shore,

And though war's missiles fell like rain,

He ever passed above the slain.

Hence many thought some Unseen Power

Protected him each woeful hour.

Be as it may, it seems that fear

Had never whispered in his ear.

He lived aloof, what vengeance made,

A daring Northern renegade.

He cared not for the Southern Cause,

He cared not for man's puny laws,

He fought for vengeance, and his foes

Fought 'neath the Union flag. His woes

Were great, for all he loved had gone

To that strange bourne where phantoms wan

Hold mystic rites—life's secrets learn,

For which all truly great souls yearn.

Aye! those he loved with all his heart,

With all his soul, in their blood fell

By Jennison and clan—the cruel smart

In his breast rankles like a hell.

Once, in Jennison's command,

He rose above the ranks, soon earned,

Because the leader of the band

Saw Quantrell knew more than he e'er had
    learned

Of war's black art—yet did betray

The greatest trust that cheers life's day.

Those he promised to protect he slew,

Would number Quantrell with the dead,

But fate decreed through him should rue

His foes that they his dear ones' blood had
    shed.

Yet Quantrell, with a conscience keen,

Knew if he could he 'd rather been

A soldier on the Northern side,

But fate and vengeance this denied.

All through the war his thoughts upbraid

That he lived on a renegade—

As when, by God from home and Heaven

Ambitious Satan, distant driven,

Far on solitary went,

And far through space his journey bent,

With thoughts full bitter with defeat,

And a remorse pride could not cheat,

That he had with his Father warr'd,

And with his brother, Christ, our Lord—

Though swift through dread immensity

He flies the boundless, bottomless sea—

Passing o'er frozen, o'er fiery worlds,

Past burning meteor as it hurls—

Expecting to some realm obtain,

Where he might e'er unrivaled reign,

Still he heart-sick with dark thoughts vain.

'Though Quantrell thus unhappy, he

Kept hidden all his misery—

Provoked to vengeance, his loved slain,

A Nemesis he roam'd the plain.

Thus hatred overpowers well

All other passions, like a hell.

He thought with feelings dread, aghast,

Death ravished all the golden past,

Which was so bright—too bright to last!

One panacea alone he found,

In war's dread thunders echoing round!

"Pool! post a guard on yonder hill,

And then we 'll try and get our fill

From this old farmer's well-stocked farm!"

The guard is placed to watch for harm—

They hasten—enter through the gate,

Where earth seems not so desolate

As most spots where the iron feet

Of war had trampled down unmeet.

The farmer came unto his door

And hailed them as a friend of yore—

This a surprise, and, too, a foil,

A foe each thought he would despoil.

When the bold chief had seen the man,

And closely did his features scan,

And with him talked, he knew the truth,

That Harris was a friend, forsooth.

" Dismount!" the mighty chief did say,

Which to the word all did obey.

Beneath the farmer's broad, wide roof,

Which knew the mingled warp and woof

Of happier days, the guerrillas came,

Ate of the store the farmer's dame

Prepared, assisted by her daughter fair,

A ripe brunette of beauty rare.

Oh! she was wondrous, passing fair !

And she was happy—debonair—

A spirit she of fancy wild—

A dreamer was this lovely child.

But summers seventeen had flown

Since she had come, one of God's own :

She 'd heard the golden laugh of Flowers—

Heard step of silver-footed Hours

As they on walked the mystic heights

Of the mornings, noons and nights.

Beneath the moon's and stars' soft light

She 'd heard the voices of the night

Go sweetly laughing back to God,

As she, the child of nature, trod

The forest path o'er sand and sod.

The past to her was like a dream—

The present hers—the future's beam

She knew not—it is well, I trow,

That future 's hard and full of woe.

Alas! how short the sight of man !

The vail o'er hours to come none scan—

The past lives o'er, a memory,

The future a sweet flower of hope—

The present is a flower we see—

Few tend, while many see it mope;
Aye! let it pass, and when afar,
Like child that weeps to grasp a star,
They weep for years they threw away.
Time God doth lend man that he may
Rise from the earth in higher air,
And bloom in beauty bright and fair!
The outlaws all enjoy the hours
Spent midst wines and vines and flowers.
Behold the ruby wine they pass,
It flames and dances in the glass!—
Hark to the song that John McKeene
Sings to guitar the young girl plays—
By nature singing his, I ween,
In song a talent he displays:

"Give Heaven the good, and Hell the bad,
    Yield me the lovely and the fair,

For though my heart be sick and sad,
    A girl's sweet face dispels my care.
Drink! drink the rosy, sparkling wine
To woman, lovely and divine.

" Oh! what's the poet's lofty wreath
    To the wreath of a fair maid's arms,
Encircling you, when she doth breathe,
    Her deep love gemm'd by all her charms!
Then drink the rosy, sparkling wine
To woman, lovely and divine.

" Then drain the foaming, sparkling glass
    To her who brings such peace and bliss;
Whose tender eyes we cannot pass
    Without we long to woo and kiss.
Drink! drink the rosy sparkling wine
To woman, lovely and divine."

When he had closed, fair Annie's eyes
Sparkled with a sweet surprise.

The singer was a handsome man ;

The maiden did his features scan

Till she found his eyes on her,

Then she blushed to find they were.

Her heart was not a frozen lake

On whose cold brink fond Cupid stands,

But it was warm, like winds that wake

In June, blown from the Southern lands ;

And April showers of affection flowed

From her summer heart of tender love,

Through her soft eyes which sweetly glowed

With beauty of the light above.

This love we sometimes see, apart,

Alone, forever glowing fresh and new—

A flower that grows from God's great heart—

A love, fair, radiant, sweet and true.

    *   *   *   *   *

Low sinks along the purple hills,

Which shadow vale of flower and rills,

And gives the forest black and dun

The aspect of a thing to shun—

That its dense wilds do deep afford

The stronghold of a robber horde—

The setting sun, and softly glances

Farewell to earth as night advances.

Said Quantrell, when he and men-at-arms

Left their hospitable friends. " If harms

Thy foes one single hair, good sir,

Of yours or your good folks, I swear

To make them rue the hour they came

To do thee wrong—so sure my name

Is Quantrell. Though deemed a ghoul,

God knows I am not near so foul—

Thought wretch on earth, astray from
    Heaven,

Who lost the route that God had given—

I have one virtue 'midst my crimes—

I have a grateful heart all times ;

Who my dark hours tries to make less

Will ever find me in distress

A friend—and never be it said

When needed most I ever fled,

Though foes unnumbered trod him down

And all the world gave him a frown.

Though warring with enemies that claim

A love for the United States,

I've naught against the Union's fame—

A victim I of all the fates!

Ohio* is my natal home—

Fate forced me from that land to roam!

A twin—my brother slain, and all

I dearly loved—their ghosts now call

For vengeance from the hills and vales—

Hark! now I hear their mournful wails!

The South outlaws me—doth ignore—

Because I will not spare a foe

* Canal Dover, Tuscarawas Co., Ohio.

Of those who brought forevermore

A bitter and eternal woe.

Aside from those who wrought my woe

In mercy I've spared many a foe.

Well! as for the South I've no love at all,

The Confederacy, soon, aye! soon must fall!—

I stand alone!—I'm not afraid!—

An outlaw and a renegade!"

"Farewell!" he said—each man's good-by

Is spoken in a hand toss'd high.

O'er each guerrilla's head defined

His black plume nodded in the wind.

They hasten on—their friends' kind eyes

Follow them along the skies.

Lo! Luna rises soft and bright

Above the battlements of night!

O'er outlaw'd loveliness of wilds

Where fairest forest flower smiles.

Lo! see upon yon great hill's height,

Beneath the floating moon's pale light,

The guerrillas!—giant ghosts appear!

Those warlike phantoms mortals fear!—

Seen but a moment in the mist!

Then pass like shades the sun hath kiss'd.

       *   *   *   *   *

The soft round moon did yet blush red,

Like beauteous rose above the dead—

And the lamps the saints hang out

For freed spirits on their route

To Heaven, burned bright across the skies

And lit far space to mortals' eyes—

When, like ten thousand demons driven,

That have no hope to be forgiven,

There rose a mad and mocking yell

That sounded like a burst from Hell!

Piercing the deep wolds through and through,

And sweeping the wide prairies too—

Jayhawkers came, and came Redlegs,

Hearing how Harris had oped his kegs

Of wine, his cupboard, his larder all,

To Quantrell and men, and this did call—

This outrage to the Jennison cause,

Swift punishment by outlaws' laws.

A dark form neared the Harris home,

And call'd: " Halloo! halloo! to the door come!

I'd speak to you and ask advice!"

The farmer answered in a trice.

But scarcely had he oped the door,

When he fell dying on the floor,

And loud report of carbine shot

Rang on the night air round the spot!—

In fear the wife and daughter go

Hastened to Harris, while their foe

Fired the house—saw it consume

To what was called " the Jennison tomb."*

---

* The term applied to the remains of the houses burned
by Jennison.

Mother and daughter see the doom,

And with the wounded man they fly

To a neighbor good and nigh,

Where soon the wounded man did die.

The rough riders, led by Jennison,

Follow'd Quantrell and men with knife and gun,

And when they overtook that clan,

It was a battle every man

Of them will ne'er, will ne'er forget,

Though dews of five-score years do wet

His brow—for it was fierce and hot,

And angry poured the whistling shot!

And savagely foes hand to hand,

With their knives stained with blood the sand.

Of those who fought in furious rage,

Many were young on life's strange stage—

Some had reached the winter of their age:

All mingled in the battle-cloud,

While thundered the voice of conflict loud!

As fierce the fight as Wilson Creek,*

Where the dead fell fast and thick.

With ensign " Quantrell," a black flag high,

Proudly flaunted the smoky sky—

While the Union flag streamed out,

O'er Red-leg and Jayhawker rout.

The serried ranks of friend and foe,

Fought hand to hand and toe to toe.

The war-horse rears and strikes as fierce

As rider, whose sharp bowies pierce

Quivering flesh and harder bone —

When fall the mighty with a groan.

It was a fierce and awful fight!

The men that died in battle great,

They fought as demons in Hell's light,

For some poor fickle boon of fate—

* The Battle of Wilson Creek, which was a glorious victory for the Union forces, 5,000 of them whipping 20,000 Rebels.

Hell's light, so dreadful in its glare

It makes e'en darkness welcome there.

Yells rose to th' anxious, listening stars!

Near kindred to the Great Unknown—

They sank until Hell's great gate jars,

And Satan startles on his throne!

As oft, here Quantrell plainly showed

Why his feared name was dreaded so—

Why his savage fame e'er redder glowed

'Long Border, wheresoe'er men go.

While foes his death forever sought,

To lay him bleeding on the sods—

He handled weapons quick as thought

And sent them howling to their gods!

As down the midnight depths of Hell

A fiend is hurled by unseen hands—

A fiend that dared to mock God, well

Forever falls, and he never lands!

Fierce Quantrell's joy and his wild cry

Whene'er a foe dead, dying fell,

Is as when a fiend soars t'ward the sky

Above the sombre clouds of Hell.

"'Tis useless that the just assail!—

It seems the fiends these days prevail!"

Cried Jennison, when Quantrell fell

Upon his squadron like a hell;

Till, vanquished, he afflicted grieves

O'er troops now scattered like the leaves!

For few that lived, with him had fled,

Leaving their many unburied dead

With Quantrell and the men he led.

   * * * * *

When John McKeene knew all the truth

His heart was touched with tender ruth

For her, the black-eyed girl he loved,

From whom he, war compelling, roved.

With a short leave of absence, he

Returned to her he longed to see.

He found her, and he vowed to take

Swift vengeance on their foes, and make

The murderers of fair Annie's sire

Deep rue the deed.   'Twas her desire

To part no more with her fond lover,

Though he lived an outlaw rover.

Whether the cause is right or wrong,

Or whether the man is weak or strong,

True woman goes where her heart dictates,

The rest she leaves unto the fates.

Now with her lover she agreed

To join clan Quantrell well did lead.

As McKeene's wife, 'twas thus she'd go

In war to share his weal and woe—

This she would do in man's attire.

With mutual—with a like desire,

They on good steeds a preacher found

Who married them—he on the ground

Before his door—they on their steeds.   The wife

In man's attire now changed her mode of life.

Her and her husband's honeymoon

Was passed 'mid scenes of blood: no boon

Of peace or rest was theirs—they saw

The awful import of life's law—

They realized in battles red

The beauty of that peace far fled,

That war's black art was Hell's dark plan

To feed on God's best gift to man.

  * * * * *

It is the beauteous month of June,

When the air re-echoes many a tune

The angels sing to God on high,

While basking 'neath Christ's tender eye—

When great Presences seem to dwell

On hills, in woods and flowery dell.

Great beauties may all radiant be

On Earth, which man 's too blind to see;

A thousand poems unexpressed

May be within the poet's breast,

Which angels read that wander by,

Sweet pilgrims from beyond the sky.

'Tis morn! and near Lee Summit town

McKeene and wife are riding down

The prairies green, with friends but few—

Lo! the Seventh Missouri comes in view!

But eight unto a thousand strong,

A fight begins, but lasts not long.

As Spartans fought in days of old

So fought the few guerrillas bold,

Till seven were slain : among the seven

John McKeene his life had given,

And Annie, his wife, fell in her gore,

Dire afflicted with the wounds she bore.

And when a soldier sought to slay,

She quickly doth her sex betray,

For ere he'd time her death to track

She pulled her long hair down her back

And looked at him with woman's eyes,

Which woke in him a soft surprise.

Her beauty held him like a dream—

He could not move, so fair the beam!

Like summer moon through clouds of night

She broke upon his ravished sight!—

Oh! strangely sweet her voice did seem—

Like Heaven-sent whispers in a dream!

Spoke as she lay, sad, weak and wan :

"Though all I love are dead and gone,

I'd not die yet. For Jesus' sake,

A grave for my dear dead one make!"

Hot tears ran down her cheeks so pale ;

Deep feelings caused her speech to fail

For a time, till the regiment all drew

Around her—then her words renew.

To the Colonel then she did appeal,

And found his heart was not all steel.

At her request he in a grave

Placed her dead husband, once so brave.

At her request, whom he did pity,

He sent her on to Kansas City,

Where she fell into the care

Of Sisters of Mercy, and well did fare;

And when recovered gave her hours—

Like so many precious flowers—

To waiting on the sick—on wounded

Who fell in battle sore confounded.

When the Star of Peace arose,

She forgave her bitterest foes,

And never mentioned her dark woes.

Deep in recesses of each heart

Some sacred, cherish'd secret lies,

Which tenderly is laid apart

From the world's inquiring eyes.

A Sister of Mercy at New Orleans,

Annie nursed the sick 'midst direful scenes

Of yellow fever—diseases all

Which the heart of man appal—

Till eighteen hundred and seventy-eight,

When she yielded to the blast of fate.

And Sister Celeste* (Annie McKeene)

Sleeps with the just and blest, I ween.

God never forgets the sore-tried soul,

Unknown to fame or at fame's goal—

But high in dark mysterious realm

The Mighty One directs the helm

Of all that's been, is, e'er will be,

Through time and through eternity.

* The devout Sister of Mercy who recently died of yellow fever at New Orleans, while at the faithful discharge of her duty in attending to the wants of those afflicted with yellow fever.

6

CANTO VI.

WILD BILL.

O! Phœbus climbs the hills of morn!

And white-robed day is newly born.

Far o'er the prairies, fair to see,

Wild yellow sunflowers flourish free

For miles and miles, a golden sea!

Here countless wild-flowers breast the wind,

As in Shakspeare are most thoughts enshrined

Which breathe the beauty of immortal mind.

One mile, and scarce a mile, apart,

Are now encamped two warlike clans—

But soon from their still rest they'll start,

For each prepares for battle's dread demands!

Soon shall arise the voice of war,

And death will lead the wild uproar!

As black as crime out one flag flows,

With "Quantrell" writ in red it rose;

While o'er the other, fair as light,

The stars and stripes wave beauteous bright!

Lo! those o'er whom the Union banner

Floats in such a winsome manner,

Approach their foes, whom Younger leads

To battle where the fighter bleeds.

Why was not the great guerrilla here

Whom all his foes so well do fear?

Low lying nigh a river scaur,

When ten to his one his foemen are,

Bold Quantrell waited a fierce fight.

His lieutenant, with a force bedight,

He had sent upon a scout

To forage through the land about,

Bushwhack and any foeman rout.

All suddenly Cole Younger heard

A voice—any other he preferred—

A voice, in tones so deep and loud

It seemed to pierce the trembling cloud.

From Younger's lips this warning fell:

" Boys! we're on the brink of Hell!

That sound is Wild Bill's* Border yell!"

Bold Younger to himself now thought,

"I have a foe I have not sought!

Though in my days' best fighting hour,

This foe will try my greatest power—

Try power of each and every man;

He leads a fierce and desperate clan!

I do confess beneath my breath

I dread to fight this son of death.

If Quantrell was but here, how proud

I'd rush into the battle-cloud.

Though I'm a Hector in the fight,

Wild Bill's Achilles in his might—

But, pshaw! I'll trust all to the fates—

*William Hicock, famous as " Wild Bill."

We'll war like devils at Hell's gates—

Buffalo Bill and Texas Jack,

I see, help lead the yelling pack!

These men seem devils hot from Hell,

Whom Satan seems to shield too well.

When I fought them in Texas in the past

I then swore an oath it was my last.

From what I learn they're on a scout

To spy fierce Quantrell's secrets out.

But there they're ' off,' for Quantrell's deep

And e'er doth his own secrets keep—

He ever sleeps where none can say,

Safe hid, that gold may not betray.

Boys! ere we enter in this row,

I want to tell you here and now—

That your best fighting must be done,

Or when goes down yon wandering sun

He'll look upon us dead and stark.

Gird up your loins—each weapon mark—

See that each cartridge is at hand,

And each weapon to command!

We fight Wild Bill!—he comes this way—

That means he comes to murderous slay—

It means we 'll have the devil to pay!

For Bill, the cuss, when free from liquor,

No use denying, makes things sicker—

With crew he from the wilds obtains,

His Indian-fighters of the plains—

Than any other class of men

That fate e'er on this earth did pen!

Hark! once more Bill's border yell!

Our foes are nearing—lie low well!

Down with the steeds!—in ambush, so

We 'll have advantage of the foe,

And get the 'drop' on them, I know!"

Down sink the steeds, well trained to war,

And all is still as at death's door

When death alone is there no more.

The desperate crew that Bill doth lead

Now dashes by at headlong speed—

Cole Younger's clan arise and fire,

Get a reply that none desire.

Now Younger cried, with hurried speech,

" To horse ! and for your foemen ' reach ! ' "

They mount, they charge, fire oft and well,

While Bill and boys on their ranks tell—

On each side many a strong man fell ;

Where Wild Bill fought, the dead do swell

To thrice the number elsewhere slain.

He flies, he flashes o'er the plain—

He kills before, behind, the same—

Shoots on all sides—true is his aim :

He fires with such rapidity

One stream of fire doth ever free

Flame from the mouths of his fire arms,

For each hand a revolver warms.

His thundering yells incessant rise,

Which tell his foes he them defies—

His long hair snaps and cracks behind,

And lashes the complaining wind;

He bristles like a porcupine

With weapons growling in a line—

An arsenal that spins and flies

Before the watcher's wondering eyes,

He seems to be—his thundering yell

Rising like a voice from Hell!

Savage the conflict, dread and hot—

Swift, sure and oft the fighters shot—

Oft saddles empty as men die,

Oft riderless steeds the prairie fly.

The doubtful combat they maintain

Till night's deep shades involve the plain—

When Younger sent one of his men

For Quantrell, lying in the glen

Hard by Blue River, waiting then

For Jennison's and Ewing's men.

Quantrell came at Cole's desire,

But found none on whom to wreak his ire—

Wild Bill had learned of Younger's aid,

And vanished in night's friendly shade.

CANTO VII.

YOUNGER AND HIS MEN.

EARTH clothed with grass—with each
fair thing
Of flowers—of all the gems of
spring—

In beauty dreams: thus kissed by Heaven
'Twould seem Christ's death had all forgiven.

Day blushes on the summit height,

There dwells a calm and holy still;

The warring winds that howled all night,

Soft whispers breathe upon the hill!

As bridal bark with silken sails

First leaves its moorings on Time's shore,

And happy speeds before soft gales

Adown Life's river, each explore

The blithe bird winds his dulcet horn,

Whose tones float through the depths of
morn,

For silver springs of love do flow

From his fond spirit, rich I know.

And morning broke upon a sight

Of blood and carnage of a fearful fight!

Upon Cole Younger and his men

Burying their dead deep in the glen.

When finished, all wearily sat down

To rest themselves upon the ground.

Quoth Younger: " Since foes were as great

In numbers as ourselves, our fate

Is well—aye! exceeding well,

Though many of your comrades fell.

Yet many of Wild Bill's best men

Are dead in this prairie glen.

Such, such is war—no use to weep

O'er those that woo eternal sleep—

They're gone beyond our power to keep.

To-morrow may see us as they—

God pity us every one, I say!

Well, boys! while we rest I'll tell a story,

Here on the field of battle gory,

With no disrespect to those gone to glory.

In Texas, Wild Bill, with a score

Of Indian fighters of the plain,

Were driven to a bloody war,

And many were their foes then slain.

'Twas on a time when Bill, the devil,

Went south, he said to hold the Texans level.

His followers were fifty odd,

And they were rough-and-ready shod

For any 'scrimmage' great or small.

In Shelby County—it was fall—

Two hundred thieving 'Regulators'

Came down upon them like a flash;

But soon they rued, these Texas traitors,

That they had made their reckless dash ;

So many of them in battle fell

That few were left the tale to tell.

Their bloody hurt yet rankles sore,

And since that day, they're not for war.

There man can travel, day or night,

And never find a foe to fight,

If like Wild Bill he is bedight.

To that section I refer,

Where they ' waked the wrong passenger ! '

They wakened Wild Bill and his crew,

They wakened Bill, who fifty slew.

Ah ! when he fires he misses not,

But strikes his aim—the very spot.

'Twas this that made his bristling name,

'Twas thus he got his ' drop ' on fame.

Had I not worn a steel breast-plate,

Death now would triumph o'er my fate.

Full fifty times Bill's bullets struck my breast,

Full fifty times they flattened on my crest."

Now Younger's mind being broader far

Than average partisan of the war,

He could acknowledge, and he would,

The prowess of a foe withstood.

" Well, boys ! up now, let us away—

Dawn crimsons at approach of day !

Quantrell told me Ewing and Jennison

He to-day expects—so look for fun

Down near the Blue—he ordered me

To fail not at the battle be."

He leaps upon his war·horse, light,

And spurs him t'ward the coming fight,

His followers close upon his flight.

CANTO VIII.

IN THE SNI HILLS.

ROM out the deep, on golden wings,
The blushing angel Morning springs!
And her fond smiles of beauty dwell,
On hill and plain with magic spell—
Dwell on the mist-clothed hills of Sni,
Which, tower-like, seem to touch the sky,
Deep in whose fastness Quantrell lay,
Of a hot slow fever the sad prey.
He thinks upon his years of life,
Of childhood, boyhood, manhood's strife,
And all his life's acts pass him by
Like sheeted ghosts we oft descry
When night engulfs the world with shade,
And God breathes "I watch—be not afraid!"

Among his many deeds of war,

There's one he deeply doth deplore.

Olathe, Lone Jack, other places

Gave him no pain—but one disgraces

All others—and he cursed the day

When his spy did his trust betray,

And thus made Lawrence all his prey.

He cursed his weakness at that hour

To check his men's fierce, brutal power,

Who slaughtered with a mad desire,

Inflaméd with liquor's fatal fire—

Like maddened bloodhounds in their ire.

He cursed his base and treacherous spy,

Who told to him a cruel lie—

Led him to think that those were there,

Who brought him all his deep despair.

Those who destroyed all he did cherish—

Caused in life's fairest flower to perish.

Yet there was one act which, sublime,

Should glow 'mid his dark deeds of crime—

An act of which he should be proud,

One star of beauty through the cloud.

When his wild crew of drunken beasts,

Who joyed in death's remorseless feasts,

Were glutting their mad thirst for blood,

When died two hundred mortals good—

He took some fifty men or more,

Who were in the Eldridge House before,

Them to the city's south conveyed,

Where to protect them he essayed;

He placed them in a barrack, then

With his fire-arms defied his men.

But hark! what sound of hurrying feet

Awakes the silence of the hills?

And yells that caverns all repeat,

To wind that wanders where it wills!

The fierce and cruel ghouls of war,

The ope-mouthed cannons loudly roar.

7

Forgetting all his sickness now

The great guerrilla chieftain rose,

And mounting his black steed—his brow

Is scowled—he spurs to friends and foes!

His men retreat!—He loud doth cry:

"Halt! right about! beat back the foe!"

They halt!—they charge!—on him rely

Who e'er had brought them out of woe.

"Yield not! yield not, though all the host

Of foes are led by Hector's mighty ghost!"

Though Quantrell's genius was in war,

He gave his quick commands as short

As words express—to army lore,

Not language, he ever had resort.

"'Tis strange!" he thought, "that Anderson,

The reckless Bill, should thus retreat!

That Frank or Jesse James should run,

Todd, Poole, or even Younger beat

A back track when 'tis wise they should,

When odds are met too great to be with-
    stood—

'Tis not strange, for they have wisdom good.

But Anderson! 'tis first he e'er went back,

Upon his red and bloody track."

This all through Quantrell's mind did flash,

As on his crime-hued steed did dash

The chieftain—for Anderson he'd sent out

Upon a far and dangerous scout.

The guerrillas well the fight maintain,

Since Quantrell is with them again;

His deep, defiant, thundering yell

All their wild fears doth quickly quell;

His familiar and assuring voice,

Made their once-fearing hearts rejoice,

Though outnumbered ten to one.

But where is he, Bill Anderson?

" Dead!" a guerrilla said he knew—

" Died 'mid a score of foes he slew."

On his battle-footed steed,

Quantrell e'er his force doth lead.

It is an awful, fearful fight

For neither foe will take to flight—

The dead are falling left and right.

The awful clang of conflict roars,

Shakes hills and distant shelly shores;

Like terrific thunders roll,

Flashing light from pole to pole ;

Like awful voice of the great God calling

Far through the vast and boundless deep

Of Eternity, to great soul falling

To everlasting woe to weep.

The sounds of battle echo far

Through the misty hills of Sni,

Loud thunders dread the voice of war,

And seem to shake the distant sky.

The stern Avenger—Renegade—

The guerrilla chieftain, Quantrell, fought

Coolly, which his men's fears allayed,

Who well his lion spirit caught.

Day wanes, night nears, the carnage still

Goes on—red Murder walks his direful
  rounds,

Oft blanches pale—disturbed, the hill

Trembles at war's terrific sounds.

The Red-Legs and Jayhawkers fought

With frenzy, fury, fierce and wild,

'Neath Jennison, but all for naught,

For Quantrell, the avenger, smiled

Upon his men, a potent smile—

A smile, though grim and savage like the war,

His men from it took hope the while,

And, cyclone-like, their foes before

Them, their red hands of vengeance hurled,

As leaves by storm are swept across the world.

CANTO IX.

GENERAL EWING'S CAMP—THE POET.

HE breath of spring, soft, fresh and
 rare,
 With fragrance sweet of unknown
flowers,
Comes wafting through the yielding air,
And bathes with love the hazel bowers.
One who wore the scallop shoon,
Who lingered yet in life's fair noon,
Was pacing as a sentinel,
Before a tent, white, wide and tall;
Where General Thomas Ewing slept—
Above, the stars their vigils kept.
Ewing liked this child of song,

Who could tell adventures long

In the richest flowing rhyme—

Romances of a bygone time,

And he sang of deeds sublime.

E'en things uncanny, dark and dull,

From his refining crucible

Reflected fair and beautiful!

And everything, crude though it be,

Came from his soul in beauty free!—

In liquid, musical numbers given,

As though Christ handed joys from Heaven.

The poet's heart was full of woe:

She, whom he loved, who loved him so.

The daughter of his country's foe,

Was distant, in the South afar—

And her near kin his foes all are.

But deep within his heart he swore,

He would have her though the roar

Of thousands of war's missiles dire,

Poured their deadly heated fire.

"She's mine!" he said; "the danger's great—

But love the greatest odds defies.

Who would not dare both death and fate,

To win so sweet, so fair a prize!"

He owned a steed—one of a few—

Which mighty deeds of speed could do;

With this swift courser, and fire-arms,

He ventured to defy all harms,

And bear the lovely girl away,

Who pined in secret for the day

When the child of song would come,

And bear her from her hateful home.

He wooed her with the poet's power

Of love, that blooms a heavenly flower.

He told her that perchance her name—

Her love for him, one beauteous flame,

With his—would live in song and fame;

For greater than kings, with kingdoms strong,

Are the mighty kings of song.

Kings and kingdoms pass away

In time, as snow 'neath sun's hot ray,

But the true bard's verse will live alway,

Like one eternal summer day.

She listened to his songs of love,

And hence was lost to all save him ;

His poems burned like stars above,

Like magic worked on woman's whim.

His song could win e'en Amazon's heart.

Who can resist the poet's art,

When he hath that fine frenzy of the brain,

Which the true poet doth retain ?

There was no sin that Ethel gave

Heart, soul and all unto the brave

And noble son of silken song

Against friends' wishes !—wherefore wrong?

An angel in its flight afar—

God's messenger—may pause, nor wrong,

To list a moment to some star
Which hath immortal power of song;
Nor would God chide that angel sweet,
Though learned to love that star so meet.

*   *   *   *   *

Night on the plain! the moon divine,
Through heaven's boundless depths sails on,
Nor mist nor cloud doth stain the fine,
Fair glories, which this night doth dawn.
Oh, beautiful!   Oh, angel night!
Fair night of June, from God above,
'Twould seem that in thy holy light
E'en iron hearts would melt to love.
The poet's plans thus far work well.
'Neath window of the Southern belle,
His Northern vow he now fulfills.
With song he wakes the vales and hills,
And her, whom long his soul did mourn;
And well his singing robes adorn,

While touching soft his harp of love,

To her who longed with him to rove—

To fly to distant, happier lands:

" Dear Ethel! fair, sweet child of God,

From love's own fountain we do drink—

From love's own fountain, o'er which nod

The passion-flowers, blooming on the brink.

" Snow-bosom'd love! I love thee;

Thy kisses are more rich and rare

Than all the other mouths that be,

Of all the many rose-lipped fair.

" I see thy face in every star,

That blossoms on the field of night—

Oh, love! thou knowest I've come far,

To gaze upon thy beauty bright!

" Thy voice sweet murmurs in mine ears,

In dreams—in dreams you smile on me—

Like music of the happy spheres,
    I breathe this melody of thee.

" From clouds that float at eventide—
    Soft, purple-tinted, gold and blue—
I see one fair as God's own bride:
    She smiles! lo! darling, it is you!

" The thought-flowers of thy mind so high,
    So beauteous blush far o'er earth's sod,
That angels wing 'twixt earth and sky,
    And carry all those flowers to God.

" A golden bell of Heaven rings now
    The matin-hour of thy sweet prime—
The flower-time of thy life, I trow,
    Is breathing odors rich as rhyme

" Of Byron—sweet as Shelley's tone—
    In their grand lays of life and love,

Dear girl ! fair girl ! thou'rt all mine own ;
  A gift, God sent me from above !

" Oh ! sweet is summer's twilight hour—
  The hour when Day sinks to his rest,
And like a weary child, each flower
  Sleeps on its Mother Earth's broad breast.

" Sweet is the star of eve, that pale
  Far glows beyond the shores of night,
When are heard the robes of angels trail
  Adown their Heaven-lit halls of light.

" But Ethel ! thou art lovelier far
  Than twilight hour with dreams so fair—
Than star of eve—than angels are
  E'en though their radiant beauty 's rare.

" Oh ! beautiful is womanhood—
  Oh ! lovely all God's girls, I trow,

And thou, dear one, of all the brood
    Art far the fairest one I know.

" Dear one! so like a rose you seem,
    Sweet blushing lone in woods afar,
Accept this rose I pluck'd in dream,
    From sweet land nestled by a star.

        [Here a rose is thrown into the maiden's window.]

" Oh, rose-lipped, rich-lipped one!
    Kissed with the dewy wine of love
I burn to clasp thee as the sun
    Burns for the loveliest star above!

" Oh, Ethel! ope thy sweet white arms—
    To thy rich bosom draw me, dear!
Where midst thy Paradise of charm
    All beauteous things and Heaven appear!

" In dreams I 'm kiss'd by thee, who smiles ;
   Though thou art far, sweet memories
      wreathe—
Though we be parted by long miles,
   Sweet odors of thy soul I breathe.

" The music and the poetry,
   Oh, Love ! of thee, sweet being, near,
Is sweeter than all else to me,
   More lovely and more dearly dear.

" When left with thee and God, oft I,
   Deep love-drown'd by thy charms so rare,
Do pluck the star-flowers from the sky
   And place them in thy silken hair.

" Oft gaze down in thy star-lit eyes,
   See thy sweet, gentle spirit smile—
And linger there, in Paradise,
   Afar from everything that 's vile.

" The rose that thy cheek blushes fair,
　A poem blooms all poets greet—
Which kindred angels of the air
　Read with delight, for it is sweet.

" Would I were a dream in thy fond breast—
　What dearer heaven could there be!
I then would be forever blest,
　From every secret sorrow free.

" Ope! ope thy milk-white arms to me—
　Caress me with thy kisses warm—
Swoon on my kiss alone for thee,
　While I clasp thy blushing form.

" I feel thy breath, like breeze of south
　With flower-sweets laden, kiss me warm—
Oh, come! I die to kiss thy melting mouth,
　And clasp thy fair and rosy form!

" Come ! let me sink and dream and rest,.
  O Queen of angels ! sweet and fair ;
Upon the heaven of thy breast,
  And fondly love thee ever there.

" Ethel ! my beautiful ! mine own !
  To look upon thy face inspires
Sweet dreams I ne'er before have known
  And kindles all love's sacred fires.

" My burning love my soul will scorch
  If thou dost not hasten to my side,
It will consume me like a torch
  If thou art not soon my blushing bride.

" For every moment kept from thee
  Is bliss that's lost forevermore—
A gulf of sorrow unto me,
  Where waves in fury lash the shore.

8

" You look so fair I deem it true
    You bathe in dew of Heaven-grown flowers
Which God did plant Himself for you
    About his angel-builded bowers.

" On purple pinions, wing the Hours—
    The happy Hours—happy since you see
        them fly—
And lovelier are the beauteous flowers
    Whene'er they know that thou art nigh.

" Sweet Ethel ! fairest flower of love !
    Oh, fairest flower of womanhood—
I deem there 's not in Heaven above
    Another one so fair, dear, sweet and good.

" The perfume of thy love for me,
    Is sweeter than scent of rose so bright,
Though queen of all the flowers that be,
    It has not the sweets which thy charms unite.

" A single word of thine, dear one,
    Is lovelier far than voices singing,
Of all the angels Heaven doth own
    When round God's milk-white throne they're
        winging.

" In the deep clear Heaven of thine eyes,
    O lovely music-footed maid!
I see the joys of Paradise
    And feel to highest Heaven I've strayed.

" I never lived until I knew thee
    For I never loved before—
I used to walk the earth, but free
    I now along the skies do soar.

" Oh, Morning Star of all my love!
    A sea of glory dreams afar,
When I behold thee, my sweet dove,
    With beauty fairer than the star.

" And when I feel thy loving kiss,
   A golden glow of happiness
Steals through my soul—it is a bliss
   That language, dear, fails to express.

" With sweetest words that love can frame
   In poetry, e'er I'll sing thy praise—
Aye ! I shall garland thy dear name
   With beauteous, melting, lovely lays.

" Oh, it shall e'er be my delight
   To guard thee waked and in thy dreams,
I'll kiss thee to thy rest at night
   And watch thee till the morning beams.

" The hours I pass with thee, dear one !
   Are silken hours of peace to me,
When flowing streams of sweetness run
   Through all my soul with melody.

" The fair blush of thy blooming years
   Doth fill my days with golden gleams—
And wrapped in sleep 'tis you endears
   And fills my nights with beauteous dreams.

" Oh, Ethel! in thy sweet young years
   You bloom, 'midst all the fairest rose—
You keep those sweets for me with modest
     fears,
   You would not to the world disclose.

" When I thy circling zone embrace
   And kiss thy lips for me alone—
My heart, my soul, my being trace
   Thy goodness which but Heaven can own.

" When sad o'er buried hopes I grieve
   Beside a lone, neglected tomb,
As summer sweet, serene as eve,
   Thy smile makes all my being bloom.

" Thy eyes light up my soul of gloom
    As Earth lights 'neath the kiss of Heaven—
And life flowers t'ward a perfect bloom—
    Flowers fair like soul by Christ forgiven.

" When Morn her eyelids open wide
    And glances on the world below,
E'er I long to have thee by my side,
    The fairest of the flowers that grow.

" When day walks o'er the gulf of Time,
    As Christ walked o'er the happy sea,
E'en midway in the hours sublime,
    My yearning soul goes out to thee.

" When comes the hour King Sol doth pray
    To God—far in the west, ere fled—
Ere sinking down in ocean gray
    To sleep among the mighty dead,

"I long for thee, sweet star of night!
    And hearken to the roving hours,
That whisper of thy beauty bright
    And lovely Hope's delightful flowers.

"Dear Ethel! strangely dear to me,
    You float my day and nightly dreams,
Like some fair star we ever see,
    That on us down from heaven beams.

"Oh, Ethel! dearest, darling love!
    I 'll love thee while the years increase—
Thy beauty comes where'er I rove
    And brings me pleasure, hope and peace.

"Oh, when I sip of thy sweet lips
    The purple wine of love I quaff—
I heed not time though by it slips,
    For through me the sweetest pleasures laugh.

" Mine angel! thou hast all my heart,
  Yes, all my deep love, dearest one!
There's no world to me from thee apart—
  Thou art my bright star, moon and sun.

" Oh, noble, lovely, loving girl,
  Rest, rest secure that I am thine,
Throughout life's wild and stormy whirl
  I'll love thee with a love divine.

" Of all other fair ones I have chanced
    To meet, I've thought each time, 'tis she
      I've sought!
But when I in each soul advanced
  I've found a waste where there was naught.

" No flower of fragrance blossomed there—
  Each soul was like a fair sad tomb,

Which stands in snowy blank despair,
    With no sweet rose and no perfume.

" But when I found thee, then I cried
    In joy, for well I knew thy soul
Was blushing with sweet flowers denied
    To others—I had reached the goal.

"The acme of all that is to love
    Thou art—and now is blessed my ardent
        heart,
For one angel from her home above
    Did come, like God, ne'er to depart.

" Hope breathes in beauty sweet and fair,
    Of when thou'll nestle by my side—
When thou art—to whom none can compare—
    Mine own, my loved, my beauteous bride.

" In dreams upon thy beauteous breast,

    Then let my feverish being sleep

Fore'er, for I am weary and would rest

    Where cares are not, nor shadows keep."

When closed his song, the loved and fair

Young girl was breathing swift and deep ;

She longed to fly with him who dare

For her brave the dangers war doth keep.

Down from her window by a rope

She swung, his eager eyes to charm—

Swift as wing'd Love keeps pace with Hope

She in her lover's arms fell warm.

" They come !" she cries—" Dear Tom, make

    haste."

No time is lost ! away their steed now paced.

" Thy song was sweet ! Oh, sweet indeed—

But it wakes those I wish did not heed

Thy sweet, thy pure, thy lovely lay !

Oh, Tom! oh, dearest Tom, away.

Around us, all around, where my eyes turn

They come! I see their torchlights burn!

Oh, Heaven! surrounded on each side

Their stern, fierce faces now deride—

They 've sworn I shall not be thy bride!"

Her eyes burn through her silken veil,

Where passionate love doth sweet prevail—

Her vermil lips, ripe, rich and sweet,

Melt on each other when they meet.

Those luscious lips in sweet repose

Bloom on her face a breathing rose.

Her breath like that fair flower as sweet,

It charms each zephyr it doth meet.

Her swelling bosom panted high—

Her soul's warm passion through her eye

Came melting, as she her lovely head

Laid on breast of him with whom she fled.

As you gazed upon her charms, you felt

With her own sweetness she would melt!

Lovely as moonlit Venice dreams

The ages by, so beautiful she seems!

Oh, Heaven! how fair! what language tell

A beauty so remarkable!

The poet sees they 're hemmed in quite,

And sees no way to pass in flight,

How, with his lovely burden, fight!

Thrice now his raven stallion neighed—

Thrice now his hands on weapons laid.

A new thought strikes him: he would try,

And pass high o'er his foemen nigh—

His steed, which doth pursuit defy,

Could leap proportionately high.

He told his plan to her who lay

Upon his breast, like Hope at day,

Shot defiance from his midnight eyes—

Swift as a flash away he flies

With her, the lovely and the fair—

Swift as a flash they cleave the air—

They pass the heads of those below,

They leave behind the following foe.

His steed, one 'midst a million horse,

Had mighty lungs of iron force—

As occasionally great power of mind in man

Accomplishes what no other can—

Does that which others dare not try ;

He wins—they gaze with wondering eye !

While other steeds fagged in the chase,

He onward hastened in his pace ;

While others grew weary, weak and hot,

Far o'er the ground he swiftly shot.

He seemed a gift from God—a boon

To him who wore the scallop shoon.

The thunder-footed courser fled

Like some great phantom from the dead.

Did all men well his swift steed know

Who would heed the flying foe !

The radiant Ethel Trekce sleeps,

She knows she's safe with him who keeps

Her in his arms, and she feels bless'd—

Wearied from the flight she sinks to rest.

As there she lies, so sweet and white,

Kiss'd by her lover, God and night,

Her lover cries : " Oh, ere I met thee, dear,

Heaven had everything to fear—

A fair bark thou, by tempests toss'd

In dangerous waters lone and lost—

'Midst black poison-weeds one pure white
     rose—

A lamb 'midst wolves—all, all thy foes !"

On—on they dash, the tall pine trees

Pass by them like a long blue breeze—

His raven stallion, black as night,

Passes swift along like storm in flight ;

Thunders along like some vast train—

He knows the way, and so has rein.

On—on through night—o'er plain and hill,

Past mountains, where the wolf his fill

Of howling pours to the ear of night,

Which oft the great-eyed owl doth fright—

Who wings his sullen flight anigh,

The flying triune passing by.

Trees, rocks and mountains whirling seem

By them as if it is a dream.

Like voice of sad and troubled deep,

The moaning night-wind strikes the ear,

As if some mournful ghost doth weep,

Remorsefully for its earth-career.

Dim in the clouds, the hills above,

Strange, weird phantoms seem to move,

And shadow lake, long, wide and deep,

Whose waters lie in glassy sleep.

Bright Orion and the Bears give light,

From the cloudy shores of night.

"Star-whispering night! canst thou not tell

Life's secret to my yearning soul?

Canst thou not tell me where doth dwell

The great God at the highest goal?

A sentence from the golden lips

Of yonder star so fair and bright,

Might wisdom shed to man, who dips

The blackened waters of earth's gulf of night;

Yet like a melody far fled

God still is silent on the mountain-head.

Oh, this will be till He appears

Far gazing o'er the countless years.

Wake! wake! sweet maid, for in my breast

Thou hast waked a wish that will not rest,

Until those brilliant burning eyes,

Have oped on me a sweet surprise.

Wake! lift those lids of loveliness,

That thy holy gaze my soul may bless—

And with me listen to the sea,

Which speaks like a tender memory!"

She wakes! love's blush is on her cheek,

Red as the rich and rosy wine,

And sweetly from her eyes do speak

A beauty that is all divine—

A beauteous love that lives sublime—

That lives beyond the reach of time,

Like flowers immortal, fair and sweet,

That bloom in Heaven at Jesus' feet.

On—on they dash—scenes rude, fair are

By them swift traversed, then left afar—

Now through a moonlit valley sleeping

Beneath a robe of fairest flowers,

While far above star-souls are peeping

Down on earth and the mortal hours.

The Hours have chased the stars away,

There blushing comes the stepping Day,

As Night's skirts trail far down the skies,

Fading 'neath the watcher's eyes.

Lovely flowers the earth adorn

9

Under lifted eye-lids of the morn.

The opal-colored morning calls

Blithe birds and happy madrigals.

Now Tom Reworb, the poet, thought

On life, on man—on what man wrought—

His aims, ambitions, and desires—

Again his Ethel sleeps—she tires

With the long ride—'tis well! when fine

She was so flowery-feminine—

For she was saved the rude fierce shocks

Of nature, where the forest mocks.

The bard all nature's beauties did absorb—

This poet strange—strange Tom Reworb—

Sent them full many folds more fair,

To shine in poesy rich and rare.

"Oh, man! thou stranger on the earth—

Forever restless from thy birth,

Thy love, oh, wretch! for what thou hast not,

Makes life through foiled hopes a hapless lot,

Through life, love of fame's a quenchless
    fire,
In death fame's a rose o'er the dead's desire !
Each great man marks where'er he trod
In his pathway up to God.
Who tells a pure truth real and clever,
Tells it to the world forever !"
The dreadful gallop of his steed
Is like a tempest great and vast—
The bright sparks from his hoofs do bleed
Like stars unnumbered flying past—
So fast the bard starts from his dreams
A moment, then renew their beams :
" Each breeze that blows across the brow
Bears something of God's wealth of love—
Oh, garner what He yields you now,
And profit by it wheresoe'er you rove.
The sky, so soft above the earth,
Is vail of blue God spreads between

Man's world and where angels have their
    birth --

Angels that see man, by man unseen.

Is this the noon of earth ?—its prime ?

Is this man's hour, elate and wise ?

Or do we live in that sad time,

'Midst wreck of earth's fair Paradise ?

Greater than conqueror or king,

The Thinker on his throne of Thought

A scepter wields—puissant thing—

By which mutations great are wrought.

As lover clasps his leman dear,

All trembling with the joy she gives,

The Thinker, when his thought grows clear,

So shakes for joy, he knows his great thought
    lives.

The true bard's poems ne'er will die,

For God inspires them from on high—

When earth, time, man have passed away,

Heaven's angels will his songs essay.

In eternal bloom the true bard's flowers—

Flowers of thought—forever blush,

And hope walks smiling in the bowers

Where youth, love, joy are ever fresh

As glorious Shakspeare's mighty name

Stars the skyey heights of fame.

Christ's life is a poem more sublime

Than any given unto rhyme.

There are dark times when naught can bless

The poet—a sense of loneliness,

E'en midst the press of outward life—

When doth awake the inner strife

Of soul with unseen powers that be,

To learn life's strange, strange mystery.

There e'er seem hues of tender grief,

Like yellow on the autumn leaf,

In the true poet's world of Thought,

As though a breakless link is wrought

Between the feelings—the desires—

Of the poet, who aspires,

And his powers to rise and soar

O'er clouds that shut him from God's lore.

Hark! songsters waked, sing merrily

With other notes of melody!

We hear—we, of the keener sense,

Who list with hearts and souls intense—

Above earth's music, the distant melody

Of song that 's sung in Heaven eternally,

By the Immortals that God's true children be.

A song—a poem grand—and so sublime

'Tis little understood by man this side of
    time—

The greatest poet wrote it—God sublime of
    might—

All minor poets feel its influence when they
    write:

Tis this for which on earth we ever long and
    yearn,
To comprehend God's poem, the Epic of
    Etern !"
Like mighty rush of torrent goes
The jet-black courser on his way,
Far from the presence of the foes—
Earth drinks the full-blown blush of day.
And she, the silken soul of love,
Gazes in her lover's eyes above—
While he sees all of Paradise
In the deep sweet beauty of her eyes,
Where immortal light shines fair,
And clears his soul of every care.
As o'er the golden twilight sea
A voice steals like a memory
Of happy love, the bard is blessed,
When by Ethel's lovely arms caressed.
" Too fair, too pure for time's vile touch

Art thou, dear one, I love so much ;

Oh, night comes not when thou art by my
    side,

For where thou art, God doth Himself abide."

She smiles upon him as sweet morn

Smiles on a lake of shade and gloom ;

He feels her heart beat high, as borne

Along they pass amid the bloom

Of midsummer's fruits and flowers,

And fairest, sweetest sylvan bowers.

He loved her with a poet's love,

Which surpasseth angels' love above ;

Her love was like impassioned light—

A yearning, burning, steady fire ;

She threw her soul, a star so bright,

Impulsive to her heart's desire.

He kissed her rich love-wine-kissed lips ;

The burning beauty of her eye

He drank—and from her being sips

The glory of her spirit nigh.

Once more she sleeps—for she 's at peace

And happy in her lover's arms ;

His metaphysic-reveries increase,

A bard he for whom the mystical hath charms :

" The stars are tears that God once wept,

Far back, when e'en Etern was young ;

When all of life save He yet slept

In womb of Chaos yet unsprung.

His tears fell through the voidless waste

Till angels sprang to life and light,

When with their beauty charmed, they placed

Them on the garland brow of night.

The soul e'er lives—to Him goes back

From whom it came to earth and time ;

Aye ! it will live when stars grow black

And fade—souls live fore'er sublime !

Though Wrong may riot for a time

And Evil vail in robes of Good,

As o'er prose soars poetry sublime,

So Right shall rise over Wrong's black flood.

As, fashioned by the hand of God,

Yon mountain, clothed in mist and snow,

Looms o'er the clouds where none have trod

Save angels that guard man below,

So, fair in loneliness doth sleep

Yon lake's wide waters bright and deep.

God's great piercing eyes see all!

His mighty hand of awful force

Compels the dreaded storm to fall,

And guides the wandering planet's course.

Far through the clouds and storms of life

The pole-star of unburied truth

Shines bright, e'en though the selfish strife

Of some may blind their eyes, forsooth.

We fret because of limitation,

And ever yearn for far progression:

Perchance when God opens the gates of Truth

With the golden key of eternity,

'Twill prove to all His tender ruth

In vailing earth-life with mystery!

The Universe, though great and grand,

Is held in the hollow of God's hand—

Two souls are in the poet's breast,

They e'er produce a wild unrest;

One would cling to earth and time,

One o'er the stars would soar sublime."

" Whirlwind," so named the poet's steed,

Still onward passed in wondrous speed,

While lovely Ethel slept away,

Under the rosy depths of day.

Hills, mountains, rise as the courser scours,

Higher than Ilion's haughty towers.

" The flower of life, though long or brief,

Opens its petals leaf by leaf.

Through yon forest dark and wide

Perchance lone specters ever glide—

Perchance these woods of ebon night

Conceal some fearful ghouls from sight!

Where fiends oft curse the straying light

That violates eternal night.

As ghastly as the Gorgon's head

The evil things that these forests tread.

Here the weird witches of the air

Howl round the hills and shake their hissing
   hair.

From swamp Despair where all is drear

Still blooms the lovely flower of Hope

To all who yield not unto fear,

But with the worst that comes will cope.

I love to rove at early morn,

And breathe the scent of flowers rare,

When Summer, Spring's fair child, is born,

To walk the vales a virgin fair.

I hear the mighty march of God

As he thunders through the deep!

It tells me here on earth's low sod

He doth o'er all a loving vigil keep.

The morning star of life is still

For me soft glancing on the hill ;

Yet gloom oft settles on my soul

For fear I fail the shining goal—

As Raphael found the gates of Hell

Strong barricaded by a spell,

When he was sent from Heaven to see,

How wrought the sons of sorcery.

Oh, for an atmosphere more clear

Than that of common men and things,

To soar high o'er the welkin here,

On purple, azure, golden wings !

Though I stand on a hill of golden hours,

Shall I stand on the mountain of diamond
    flowers ?

What boots it when that boon is sweet,

Unknown unto the vulgar wise,

The poet, in his soul's retreat,

Above all other things **doth prize**!

Oh, God! shall open-throated war

O'er this fair land much longer roar?

I hope, ere flowers another spring

Peace will have spread her lovely wing

O'er this too-long deep-suffering land—

Oh, God! with thy almighty hand,

Hurl war and crime far in the deep,

So that we all with joy may weep!

Through eternity Truth hath no fear,

But sails triumphant Falsehood o'er,

As the immortal starry sphere

Is high above earth evermore.

Some mortals see things in dark light,

Their minds and eyes are vailed in night—

As "woman's rights" (?) are woman's wrongs—

For she who willing leaves her sphere

Throws that away which right belongs

To her and woman's lofty empire dear.

Up from the azure hills of God

A living Presence seems to rise,

And soar above the heavy clod

Of earth unto fair Paradise.

The dewdrop on yon fragrant flower

May be the tear of some sweet happy star

That weeps for joy that God's great power

Shields all creation near and far.

Oh, could the music of my lyre

Follow the high flight of my will,

To highest Heaven I would aspire,

By climbing the poet's holy hill.

Oh, life is a strange, mysterious dream,

Mingling with the day and night—

I long have tried to find that beam

Which will make all things clear and bright.

Aye! vast as night—wide as endless morn

I've restless sought life's mysterious truth

In vain—innate with me this feeling born,

Hence melancholy marks my soul forsooth.

Oh, for a land where man's spirit never mopes,

A land where roves the pure-eyed loves and
    hopes.

The nameless tumuli on shore

Of lone seas with melancholy skies,

May hold a germ, forevermore,

Of knowledge hid from wisest eyes.

Eternal whispers, breathing round,

Breathe the warm soul of other days,

I feel the import, deep, profound :

God is not far from him who prays—

When his cause is wise and just,

And he earnestly prays because he must.

I hear the bells of God !—they ring

The ending of an epoch old :

Oh, Wisdom, brood and spread thy wing

More freely o'er the new unrolled.

Great minds honor worth and brain,

Small minds to honor wealth are fain.

Who never doubted, never thought—

In conscientious doubt is power,

From such doubt the greatest things are
    wrought;

'Tis to the soul what perfume is to the flower.

Great men are numbered by no year—

The life of each immortal name

Is in the thought-prints which appear

Along the skyey heights of fame.

That I might tread the Milky Way—

Forever wander mid the stars,

I then perchance might find, some day,

A key to ope the gate that bars

The way to highest, pure, clear light,

Above earth's long and sombre night."

Like moonlight on the breast of night,

Sweetly dreaming of God's Heaven-lived light,

10

So lovely slept sweet Ethel fair,

On bosom of her lover there.

Like twilight o'er a sinless world

Her silken hair o'er her pure bosom curled ;

Her mouth is with such sweetness ripe

It doth the tenderest kiss invite.

But when they passed a holy grail,

With water filled from Heaven's sweet vale,

'Twould seem some sprinkled Ethel's face,

She woke to feel her love's embrace,

And hear throbbing of the vesper bells

Which from cathedral sweetly swells.

" Thou hast woke to give me bliss,

Dear Ethel !   Oh, thy charms inspire !

I feel immortal when thy kiss

Sinks deep into my soul of fire !

What cannot love forsooth effect ?

It drew Diana from the spheres—

Mount Ida's youth it did elect—

It holds the reign o'er endless years."

Low, soft, yet audible and sweet,

To him and Heaven she breathed his name—

Her velvet voice his ears do greet

As if from highest Heaven it came.

" Dear Tom !" she whispered, " thou art fair !"

And heaved a plaintive, ardent sigh—

" I love to breathe the virgin air

Of God, and hear the birds sing nigh.

All, everything is sweet to me

When I thy glorious image see.

These hours are sweet, these hours are fair,

Time-flowers God hands to me from Heaven—

Till I met thee my life was bare,

Since then it blooms like garden of sweet

    Aidenn."

Like seraphic music in Heaven found,

The flower-tones of her voice breathed round ;

Fair and sweet, pure as Christ's tear,

She loved her bard, warm as sun her love
    beamed ;
She trusted him without a fear,
When awake or in his arms she dreamed.
Lo ! there, in beauty 'neath the skies,
The lovers' home doth lovely rise,
And Kansas prairies meet their eyes !

CANTO X.

BATTLE OF WESTPORT.

LL summer Price had forced his way,

With his fierce army of the Gray,

T'ward north and distant setting
sun,

While Curtis, Blunt, and Pleasonton

Disputed every foot he stepped,

With Kansas men, who never slept

So sound but they remembered well

The foes that came like fiends of Hell.

And many a man of Kansas soil

Had shouldered arms the foe to foil;

They swarmed prairie, hill and glen,

To full three times ten thousand men—

Men who were fighting for their all ;

And the invaders to the wall

They swore to drive—fierce hurl them back—

Swift as a cyclone forests rack.

Price fiercely fought to Westport—there

Looked longingly to Kansas, where

He sees afar more spoils and name—

Where he thought to win a brighter fame.

But this he found a task full sore—

That fame was his, ah ! nevermore.

     *   *   *   *   *

October claims of time a share—

'Tis Sabbath morn !   Day's dawn is fair—

Though Phœbus yet is seen nowhere.

'Tis eighteen hundred and sixty-four,

And into Kansas cross Price swore

He would, that day, the twenty-third—

Hark ! voice of coming battle 's heard !

The bugle now awakes the air,

Breathing sad tones of beauty there.

The sullen tread of hosts is heard,

And neigh of war-horse fierce—the word

Of command.   All now is still,

The wind is lull'd from hill to hill.

All suddenly red flames burst out

From cannons on a breastwork high,

Behind which lay the Rebel rout ;

And iron balls scream down the sky,

And bombshells burst before, behind,

While Death and Ruin ride the wind ;

Carbine bullets shrilly sing

Dread notes of death—earth, heaven, ring !

The Federals pour their swift replies,

War's thunder mounting to the skies.

Many a strong and mighty man

Falls dead, falls dying, spent and wan.

The breastworks topple, tremble, fall !

Before shot, shell and cannon ball;

Down on each other rush fierce foes,

And dark in deadly combat close!

They close in sable clouds of smoke;

A yell bursts out which Sol awoke!

For instantly his heavy head

Up rises from his Orient bed.

And midst the roar and thunder dread,

The battle-shaken hills do groan;

A thousand ghosts of fallen dead

Shriek madly to their God Unknown!

The battle thickens—in the van,

The awful revelry of death

Would melt the hardest heart of man;

Would make him catch his faltering breath.

The fight goes on—more fearful grows;

Dun clouds of battle black the air;·

The shrieks, the groans, midst dying woes

Are mingled in war's dread despair.

The battle roars like to the blast

That drives the forest from the shore;

And thunders like the storm that vast

Sweeps Hell's great dreary regions o'er.

   *   *   *   *   *

Day wanes—the battle's o'er, and Price,

Defeated, leaves the foughten field.

The dead are heaped and scattered, cold as

  ice,

And they increase as the dying yield.

The living care for all they can,

And cheer each dire afflicted man

By some kind act or promise given,

Which smooths his way, we trust, to Heaven.

I sympathize with those who fall

Down stricken by the deadly ball,

For I have felt the cruel thing

Tear through my flesh with angry sting.

War is the worst curse of all time,

Against both God and man a crime.

Night, in her robes of mourning, sad

Comes grieving for men's passions bad—

Passions that drive the soul away

And leave naught save some bloody clay.

Here lay the bleeding trooper dying,

There lay the cause, part of a shell;

And, powder-burnt, his steed is flying

Swift from the sight where Death wrought his

    spell.

Each bird has flown, from awe is still;

The wolf, in fear, howls from the hill!

The prairie-dog barks fierce and wild,

Before his earth-house door defiled;

While his household, snakes and owls,

In earth deep, listen to his howls.

Night thickens! wolf and dog are still;

And silence broods o'er plain and hill!

Still! All still since battle-blast,

Save when some new-born phantom passed;

Lost! shrieking for some beacon light

To guide it through the starless night.

Men died so dreadful on that day,

Some of the souls that fled away,

Not vain said, of bodies thus bereft,

Were stained with blood of corses left!

      *   *   *   *   *

Oh, Muse! we now must here recite

The valor in each army there,

The brows of those who led the fight

For bravery deserve wreathed laurels fair;

So does each private soldier too,

Whether he wore the gray or blue.

The Rebels thirty thousand strong,

Their foes well-nigh as numerous throng.

McNeil, the dauntless, showed his skill

In war, and showed it with a will,

Like Hancock in the Wilderness,

His country's friend in its distress.*

Here Jennison and Ford did war

With troops that oft had heard the battle
    roar;

With his brigade, Moonlight,† the brave,

To Price defeat, his prowess gave,

As two days before that Rebel crew

He fought upon the Little Blue.

* General Winfield Scott Hancock.

"On the 7th (May 7, 1864), General Grant moved his army around Lee's right, and marched rapidly to seize the strong position of Spottsylvania Court-House, which would have placed him between the Confederates and Richmond. Lee at once divined his purpose, and fell back rapidly to the heights around Spottsylvania Court-House, which he occupied on the 8th. Upon arriving before this position, Grant found his enemy strongly intrenched in it, and at once resolved to drive him from it. On the 10th of May he made a determined attack upon the Confederate line, but failed to carry it. At daybreak on the 12th, a furious assault was made by Hancock's corps upon the right center of Lee's line, which was carried in handsome style."— *McCabe's Centennial History of the United States.*

† Col. Thomas Moonlight, of Leavenworth.

Here Hinton* proved to his country he was
  true.
The militia under Blair's† command
Sad havoc wrought on every hand.
Here Major Simpson ‡ battled bravely
With his Fifteenth Kansas Cavalry.
Here Walker § in front ranks did lead,
Astride of his uncertain steed.
Here fought Daniel Boone, the grandson bold
Of Kentucky's mighty hunter old.
'Twas here that Colonel Veale did well
'Gainst numerous foes, wild, fierce and fell—
His Shawnee County Regiment

* R. J. Hinton, author of the history of "The Army of
the Border."
† General Charles W. Blair, of Fort Scott.
‡ B. F. Simpson, present U. S. Marshal, March 1, 1880.
§ Col. Sam. Walker, of Lawrence, whose steed had the
disagreeable habit of going over to the enemy's lines during battle—a habit which had caused the death of several of
its owners.

Fought like vetérans of the tent—
Like veterans of the field of blood,
Who 've war and all its woe withstood;
And many a rebel felt the power—
They of the Southern host the flower—
Of these mighty men that came
Down upon them like a flame
Of Hell—these men of war, whom war called
    there,
Whom proud Topeka claimed a share.
Martin,* Bonebrake, Case and Burns,
Brockway, Williams, Huntoon were there—
Smith, Douthitt, each his laurel earns—
Which should ever shine in poesy fair.
Here Major Ross,† and his true men,

---

* Hon. John Martin, P. I. Bonebrake, present Auditor
of State, Ross Burns, A. H. Case, Judge David Brockway,
Arch. Williams, Dr. A. J. Huntoon, Jacob Smith, and W.
P. Douthitt, all citizens of Topeka.

† Ex-Senator E. G. Ross, editor *Lawrence Standard.*

Did service good for country then.

'Mid thickest of the fearful fight,

The Major spurred his steed of night—

And hurl'd hot shot on enemies,

As now his truncheon pen he plies.

Here Hoyt, the hero of the Blue,*

Fought brave and well the battle through.

Joe Shelby and his cavalcade

Here proved of death they were not afraid ;

They seldom heard a milder note

Than what came out of War's dread throat.

They wildly, madly, reckless fought,

As though life nor death to them was naught.

Here Colonel Moore † led a bold band

---

* " In the fight at the Blue, Col. Hoyt, with a portion of the Fifteenth Kansas Regiment, made one of the most gallant saber charges recorded in the history of the war."— *O. II. Gregg's History of Johnson County, Kansas.*

† Col. John C. Moore, the well-known journalist and lecturer.

Under Shelby's fierce command.

'Twas here, John Edwards * did all show,

He was the Federals' bitter foe :

'Though now he wields the mighty pen,

The bickering blade he wielded then ;

His men were brave as brave could be,

They fought and they died recklessly.

'Twas here Todd, the guerrilla, fell,

A reckless, daring child of Hell,

To whom peace seemed a waste of time,

Who gloried in the hour of crime.

Here Marmaduke his force did lead

With all the pomp of war to bleed—

Here Fagan, Cabel, Gordon too,

And Jackman, Thompson—leaders true

Unto the Southern cause—command

Troops fighting for Price on every hand.

* Major John N. Edwards, editor of the *Sedalia Democrat*, Sedalia, Mo.

Many more were there who battled well,

Which we leave to plodding prose to tell:

The report,* and Wilder's Annals, too,

Are exact enough for you.

The deeds of valor on the day

Of the battle of Westport it hath famed

As Bunker Hill is famed for aye—

As Lexington is immortal named.

     *   *   *   *   *

Ah! Price, thou wrought thine own defeat,

When thou offended thy great power,

Who best knew War's black art—'twas meet

That Quantrell had been with thee this, thy

    fatal hour.

     *   *   *   *   *

The storm of war has blown afar,

The star of peace is shining now—

"Swords to plowshares" turned now are—

* The official report of the battle.

All is as calm as Christ's meek brow.

Where once War's bloody feet did rove—

Whose red hands death on progress hurled,

Spring bowers of beauty, like Bismarck Grove,

Where mighty minds instruct the world.

THE END.